TANYA'S REUNION

by VALERIE FLOURNOY
pictures by JERRY PINKNEY

Dial Books for Young Readers New York

Published by
Dial Books for Young Readers
A Division of Penguin Books USA Inc.
375 Hudson Street
New York, New York 10014

Printed in the U.S.A.
First Edition
1 3 5 7 9 10 8 6 4 2

Library of Congress Cataloging in Publication Data
Flournoy, Valerie, 1952–
Tanya's reunion / by Valerie Flournoy ; pictures by Jerry Pinkney.—1st ed.
p.   cm.
Summary: When she and her grandmother go to help with preparations for
a big family reunion, Tanya learns about the history of the farm in
Virginia where Grandma grew up.
ISBN 0-8037-1604-4.—ISBN 0-8037-1605-2 (lib. bdg.)
[1. Grandmothers—Fiction. 2. Farm life—Virginia—Fiction.
3. Family reunions—Fiction. 4. Virginia—Fiction.]
I. Pinkney, Jerry, ill. II. Title.
PZ7.F667Tan 1995   [E]—dc20   94-13067   CIP   AC

The full-color artwork was prepared using
pencil and watercolor on paper.

In loving memory of Dad—
Chief Payton Isaac Flournoy, Sr.

V.F.

To Sophia W. and Arruth A.—
Thank you for your continued warmth and support.

J.P.

It was Saturday. Baking day. One of Grandma's special days. Tanya had just popped the last spoonful of bread pudding made that morning into her mouth when Grandma announced, "Got a card from Aunt Kay and Uncle John today. They've invited me to the farm before all the family arrives for the big reunion. And I've decided to go."

A silence fell across the dinner table. Neither Tanya nor her brothers, Ted and Jim, could remember their grandmother going *anywhere* without the rest of the family.

"Aren't *we* going to the farm and reunion too?" Tanya asked. She had been looking forward to the big family event and her first trip to a farm ever since the announcement had arrived.

"Yes, Tanya. We're still going," Papa reassured her.

"We can *all* go to the farm together *after* the boys' football summer camp is over," Mama suggested, glancing toward Papa.

Grandma sucked her teeth and sighed. "Now, what's all the fuss? My baby sister asked me to come home early. I suspect she needs help working out all the sleeping arrangements and finding just the right spot for all the history people will be bringing with them."

Tanya remembered Mama and Grandma talking about the plan to have as many items that were once part of the homestead . . . the farm . . . returned for the biggest family gathering ever!

"But, Mother," said Mama, "you were sick not too long ago. Do you really think this trip is wise?"

Tanya watched Grandma reach out and touch Mama's hand.

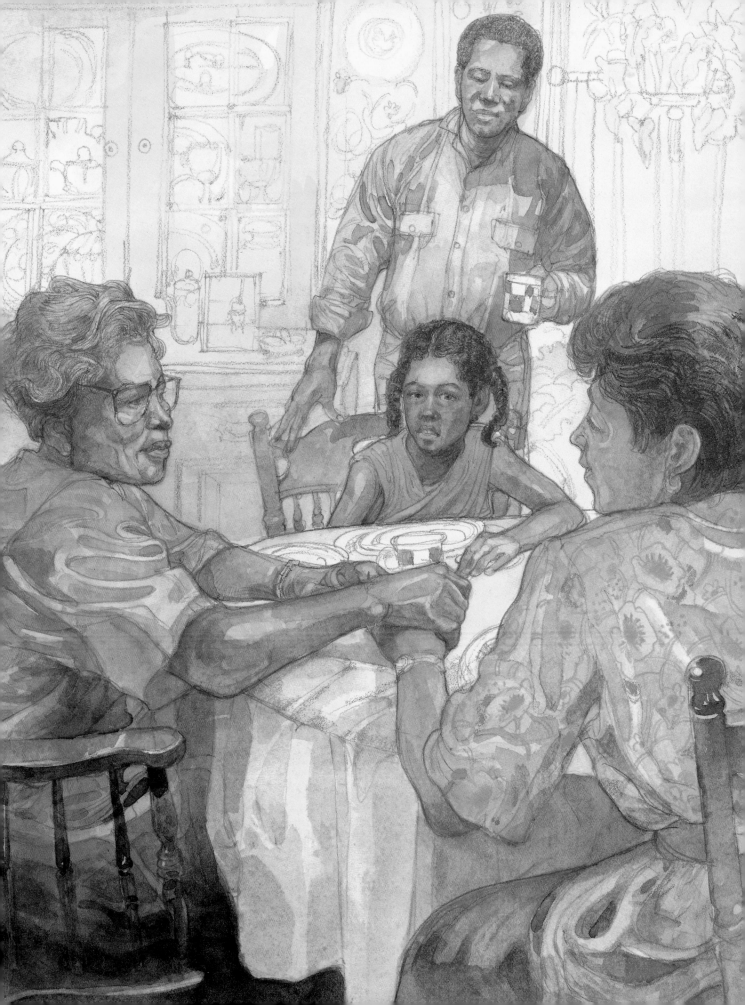

"That was then, honey, and this is now, and I'm just fine. So I'm gonna go while I'm able," the old woman said firmly. "Besides, if you're so worried about me, you can always send Tanya along to see I stay out of trouble."

A trip with Grandma! Just the two of them. Tanya couldn't believe her ears.

"*May* I go with Grandma to the farm?" she pleaded excitedly.

Mama looked from Tanya to Papa to Grandma.

"Ted and Jim *are* going to football camp," Papa gently reminded Mama. "And we *will* be joining them shortly."

Grandma pulled a letter from her apron pocket. "I think Kay mentioned some of *her* grandchildren would be visiting early too. So Tanya will have someone to play with."

Mama looked from Grandma to Papa to Tanya again. "All right," she finally agreed. "You can go."

Tanya couldn't hide the pride she felt when she saw the surprised looks on Ted's and Jim's faces.

"We've had some special days on that old farm," Grandma said with satisfaction. "And so will Tanya. You'll see."

The sun rose slowly in the morning sky as Tanya watched all her familiar places vanish behind her. Past her schoolyard and the park. Past row after row of houses and traffic lights.

And still they traveled on and on. They stopped only to switch from one bus to another. Tanya listened while Grandma spoke about "going home" to the great land of Virginia that "borned four of the first five Presidents of these United States."

And still they traveled on and on. Until the bright sunny sky grew cloudy and gray and the highway turned into never-ending dirt roads that seemed to disappear into the fields and trees, down into the "hollers," the valleys below. Tanya could barely keep her eyes open.

And still they traveled on and on . . . until finally the bus crawled to a stop.

Grandma shook Tanya gently. "We're here, Tanya honey, wake up." Tanya rubbed her eyes awake. "We're home."

Standing on the last step of the bus, Tanya spied a car, trailing clouds of dust, coming toward them. In the distance were a farmhouse and barn.

"I've been sitting for the past eight . . . nine hours," Grandma told Uncle John, who'd come to get them, "so I think I'll just let these old limbs take me the rest of the way."

Tanya watched Grandma walk slowly but steadily up the familiar roadway.

"Memories die hard," Uncle John whispered to Tanya.

Tanya wasn't certain what her great-uncle meant. She only knew that if Grandma was going to walk, she would walk too. And she raced to the old woman's side.

"Take care, honey," Grandma said. "August weather down here's meant to be eased on through, not run through."

Tanya looked up at Grandma as she stared off into the distance, a faraway look in her eyes. What Tanya saw didn't look like the pictures in her schoolbooks or magazines or the pictures in her head.

There wasn't a horse in sight and the farmhouse was just a faded memory of its original color. Tanya noticed clouds of dust floating about her ankles, turning her white socks and sneakers a grayish-brown color.

"Just open your heart to it," Grandma said. "Can't you feel the place welcomin' ya?"

Tanya didn't feel anything but hot and tired and disappointed. The farm wasn't what she expected. No, it wasn't what she expected at all.

A dog's bark drew Tanya's gaze back to the farmhouse. Stepping off the porch, a large dog at her side, was Grandma's baby sister, Kay.

"Watchin' you walk up that road, Rose Buchanan," Aunt Kay began, then gave Grandma a hug.

"Yes, on summer days like this it's as if time were standing still just a bit," Grandma finished for her.

Aunt Kay turned to her great-niece, smothering her in a welcoming hug full of warmth and softness that reminded Tanya of Grandma.

A summer breeze suddenly blew across the land, pushing the scattered gray clouds together. Tanya felt raindrops.

"Looks like it's comin' up a cloud," Uncle John said, hurrying the women onto the back porch and into the house. "I think it's *finally* gonna rain!"

Tanya was swept into the house by the laughing, talking grown-ups. Inside the kitchen Tanya met her cousin Celeste and her children, baby Adam and seven-year-old Keisha. The room was filled with wonderful aromas that made Tanya's mouth water—until she noticed the fly strip hanging above the kitchen table.

When Tanya went to bed that night, she was miserable. She barely touched her supper, until Uncle John thought to remove the fly strip dangling overhead. She missed her own room. She missed Mama and Papa, even Ted and Jim. Cousin Keisha and baby Adam were nice. But he was too small to really play with, and Keisha refused to leave her mother's side all night.

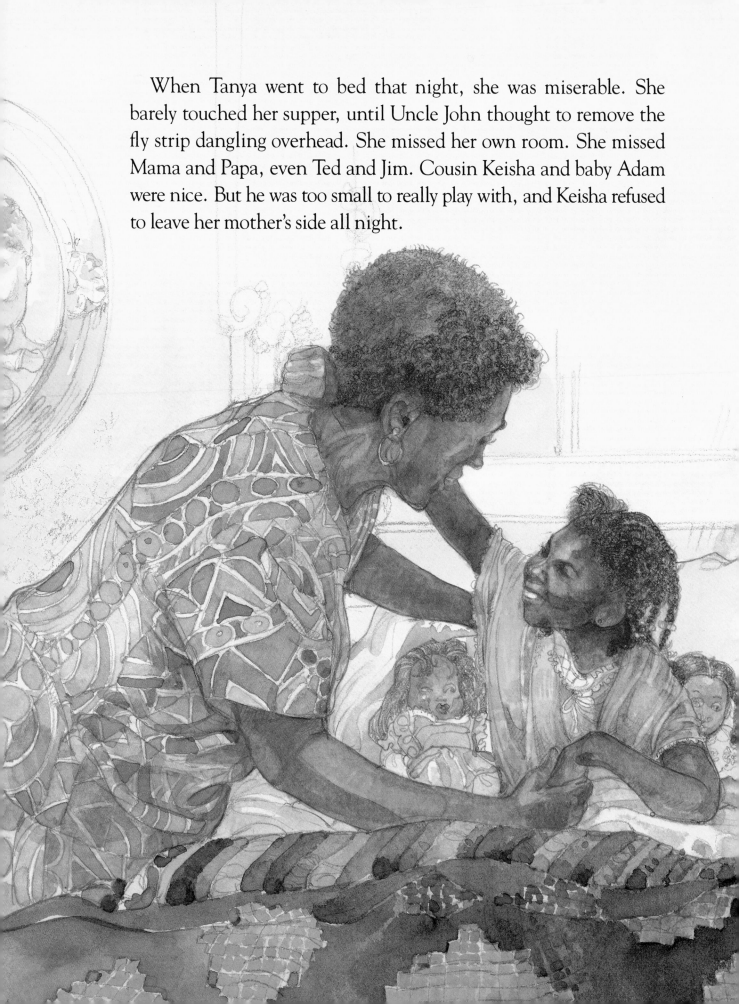

Grandma helped Aunt Kay tuck the children in. "What happened to our special days, Grandma?" whispered Tanya.

"Seems to me our first one went just fine," said Grandma. "The land needed the rain and it's finally gettin' it. Makes today kinda special, don't you think?"

Tanya sighed. "I wanna go home," she murmured into her pillow.

Cockle-doodle-do! The rooster's morning wake-up call startled cousin Keisha out of her sound sleep, and she cried until her mother came to take her into her room with the baby.

From the bed by the window, Tanya leaned against the windowsill looking over the empty farmyard. The sky was slate gray, but the air was fresh and clean and a gentle breeze swept through the window. It was also Saturday. Baking day, Tanya remembered before drifting back to sleep.

A single raindrop plopped on Tanya's face...then another...and another, until she awoke and closed the window. By the time she finished dressing, the rain sounded like a thunderous drumroll along the rooftop.

Hurrying down the staircase, Tanya stopped at the room Aunt Kay had called her sitting parlor. The room she chose to hold the family's memories. Several quilts—including Grandma's—with different colors and designs were draped across the sofa or hanging from the walls. Crocheted tablecloths and napkins, baptismal gowns and baby blankets, and a rocking chair and baby crib were also in place. There were various pots and pans, blacksmithing and gardening tools, candle molds and a few toys. Even a broom that couples jumped over when they married during slavery times. Every item was clearly and neatly labeled by its owner.

"Ahhh! Here's my northern niece. Ready for breakfast?" asked Uncle John.

"Yes! Ready!" Tanya said, turning from the doorway.

It rained through breakfast. It rained through checkers with cousin Celeste and four games of dominoes with Uncle John and Keisha. It rained through Adam's crying and Keisha's temper tantrum when Tanya hid all too well while playing hide-and-seek. It rained all morning long.

"Grandma," Tanya finally called. "Grandma, where are you?"

"In here," Grandma answered.

Tanya found Grandma, Aunt Kay, and cousin Celeste in the kitchen surrounded by boxes and lists about sleeping arrangements and who would cook what for the big reunion.

"Grandma, aren't we gonna bake today?" Tanya asked.

Grandma looked up from her lists. "Oh my," she murmured.

Tanya sighed unhappily and Grandma put her arm around her granddaughter's shoulder, leading her out the back door. The rain fell in a straight, steady stream, like a curtain separating the porch from the barnyard beyond.

Grandma patted the place beside her on the swing and Tanya slid into a familiar spot under her grandmother's arm.

"I'm sorry, Tanya honey. I guess I just plumb forgot what day this was." The old woman sighed, then laughed. "And I guess no number of stories can make you see this place through these old eyes."

"Did you *really* like living on this farm, Grandma?" Tanya asked. "Weren't you *ever* lonely?"

Grandma laughed again. "No, Tanya, I wasn't lonely. Back then, this whole farmyard: the barn, the pasture, fields, and orchard beyond"—she stretched out her arm—"this place was filled with activity. We had the land and the land had us. We worked over it, tilled and planted it. Then harvested it when it was ready. In turn the land gave us water, food, clothing, and a roof over our heads."

"If you weren't lonely, Grandma, why did you leave?" Tanya persisted.

Grandma looked out over the land, remembering. "It was after the second World War. My Isaac—your grandpa Franklin—and many other people thought we'd find better opportunities, better jobs closer to the cities up north. And we did. But we still kept the land and paid taxes on it. Sometimes let other people pay to work it, 'til Kay and John came back. But this will always be home."

Tanya and Grandma rocked slowly, silently, looking out across the rain-soaked land.

"Grandma, when you look far away. . . out there . . . what do you see?"

Grandma's eyes glowed. "I see your aunts and uncles and cousins when they lived on the farm. I see *my* father's father and his Indian bride. They built this farm so many, many years ago."

"And do you see Grandpa?" Tanya asked quietly.

"My, yes, Tanya. Your grandpa's always with me. But here on the farm he's 'specially close," the old woman answered.

The steady rain began to taper off. Grandma gave Tanya's shoulder a squeeze. "Now you, and Keisha and Adam, are a part of this farm, child," she said. "Family gatherings of this size can't happen without lists and planning and work. Everybody just pitches in and does the best they can. I know you will too."

When Grandma and Tanya returned to the kitchen, the room was in an uproar. Adam was crying loudly. The phone was ringing and the delivery man was at the door. Aunt Kay was searching for her handbag.

Grandma laughed. "Looks like we're needed."

Cousin Celeste took Adam while Grandma handled the delivery man. Tanya answered the phone and with Keisha's help found the missing box of diapers. All was calm when Aunt Kay returned with her handbag.

"Aunt Kay, may Keisha and I visit Uncle John in the barn?" Tanya asked.

"I'm sure he'll like the company," Aunt Kay said. "Just put on these old boots before you go."

Tanya and Keisha pulled on the boots and off they marched. The girls watched as Uncle John finished milking the cow. Then with his consent, Tanya sprinkled chicken feed on the ground. While the chickens ate, she and Keisha collected their eggs. After that the girls explored the barn, and when they grew tired, they climbed into the hayloft to rest.

The sun shone bright and hot when the threesome left the barn. "Weather can be right funny down here," Uncle John chuckled.

"John!" Grandma called through the screened window. "We could use some apples."

Uncle John handed each girl her own basket before pointing them in the direction of the orchard.

"Race ya!" Keisha squealed, and away she ran.

Keisha reached the orchard first. Tanya wasn't far behind when she saw something lying on the ground. She picked it up, brushed it off, and put it in the bottom of her basket before she began to pick apples.

The day slipped into dusk when the family finally sat down to supper. They had homemade apple pie for dessert—Tanya had shown Keisha how to roll the dough for the crust—topped with homemade ice cream.

Only when the last bite of pie was gone did Tanya bring out what she had found that afternoon: a piece of the fence that had once separated the farmyard from the orchard. Carved in the wood were the initials

R.B.

+

I.F.

Rose Buchanan and Isaac Franklin.

"This is *your* history, isn't it, Grandma? Yours and Grandpa's."

"Oh yes, child. A special memory of your grandpa and me," said Grandma, beaming. "We'll put it in the parlor for everyone to share."

That night Uncle John placed sleeping bags on the porch so Tanya and Keisha could pretend they were camping out. Tanya had never seen so many fireflies or heard so many crickets.

"Doesn't the farmyard *ever* get quiet?" Tanya asked Grandma, who was rocking beside her.

"Those are just night sounds, honey," Grandma said, breathing in the hot, humid night air. "Telling us all is well."

And it was.